Wake Up, Little Children

A Rise-and-Shine Rhyme

by

JIM AYLESWORTH

illustrated by

WALTER LYON KRUDOP

ATHENEUM BOOKS FOR YOUNG READERS

Wake up, little children. The day has begun.

Get out of your bed now. There's much to be done.

The old sun is rising. He's warming the air.
The breezes are stirring. They'll blow through your hair.

The wrens are all singing. They're calling for you.
The flowers are waving, still covered with dew.

The clouds will need watching. They're fluffy and white.

The hills need good children to roll them just right.

The meadow will want you. Some rabbits play there.

The grass is so soft that your feet can go bare.

The clear brook is babbling. It tumbles and flows.

The mud is awaiting the prints of your toes.

There are minnows to look for, and turtles and frogs.

Some spiders are spinning between fallen logs.

There are pebbles to toss, and monarchs to chase,

And soaring pond dragons with wings made of lace.

There are fences to hop, wild roses to smell.

A bird nest lies hidden, but you'll never tell.

Wild berries need picking. They're blacker than ink.

The old pump is waiting to give you a drink.

The woods, too, are lonesome for daughters and sons.

The trees long for climbers, and you're just the ones.

An old stump stands idle. It's waiting for you.
Sit still now and listen, as sun filters through.

The squirrels will watch you, and chatter with cheer.
The blue jays will call you. A deer may come near.

A small path will lead you back out through the wood.

You won't want to leave there but know that you should.

By the time you get home the sky will be pink.

And it will all happen in less than a wink.

So wake, little children, the day has begun.

Get out of your bed now, there's much to be done.

To summer, with love!
—J. A.

To Frieda and Pearl
—W. L. K.

Atheneum Books for Young Readers
An imprint of Simon & Schuster Children's Publishing Division
1230 Avenue of the Americas
New York, New York 10020

Text copyright © 1996 by Jim Aylesworth
Illustrations copyright © 1996 by Walter Lyon Krudop

Book design by Michael Nelson

The text of this book is set in PopplPontifex
The illustrations are rendered in oil and vinyl paint

First edition

Printed in the United States of America

10   9   8   7   6   5   4   3   2   1

Library of Congress Catalog Card Number 95–78298

ISBN 0-689-31857-X